How to Be a Mensch

by A. Monster

As told to Leslie Kimmelman
Illustrated by Sachiko Yoshikawa

Mensch: Someone who is honorable and kind—a good person. The word comes from Yiddish, a language once commonly spoken by Jews in many parts of the world.

It's hard to believe, but some
people are afraid of monsters.

It's true that monsters
can look scary.

But most of us are kind and helpful.

Monsters can even be mensches!

Because **anyone** can be a mensch.

Mensches can be young or old,
short or tall,

pink or green or even striped.

They can be sporty
or warty.

ISCREAM

Mensches can be lovers of books,

makers of mud-pies,

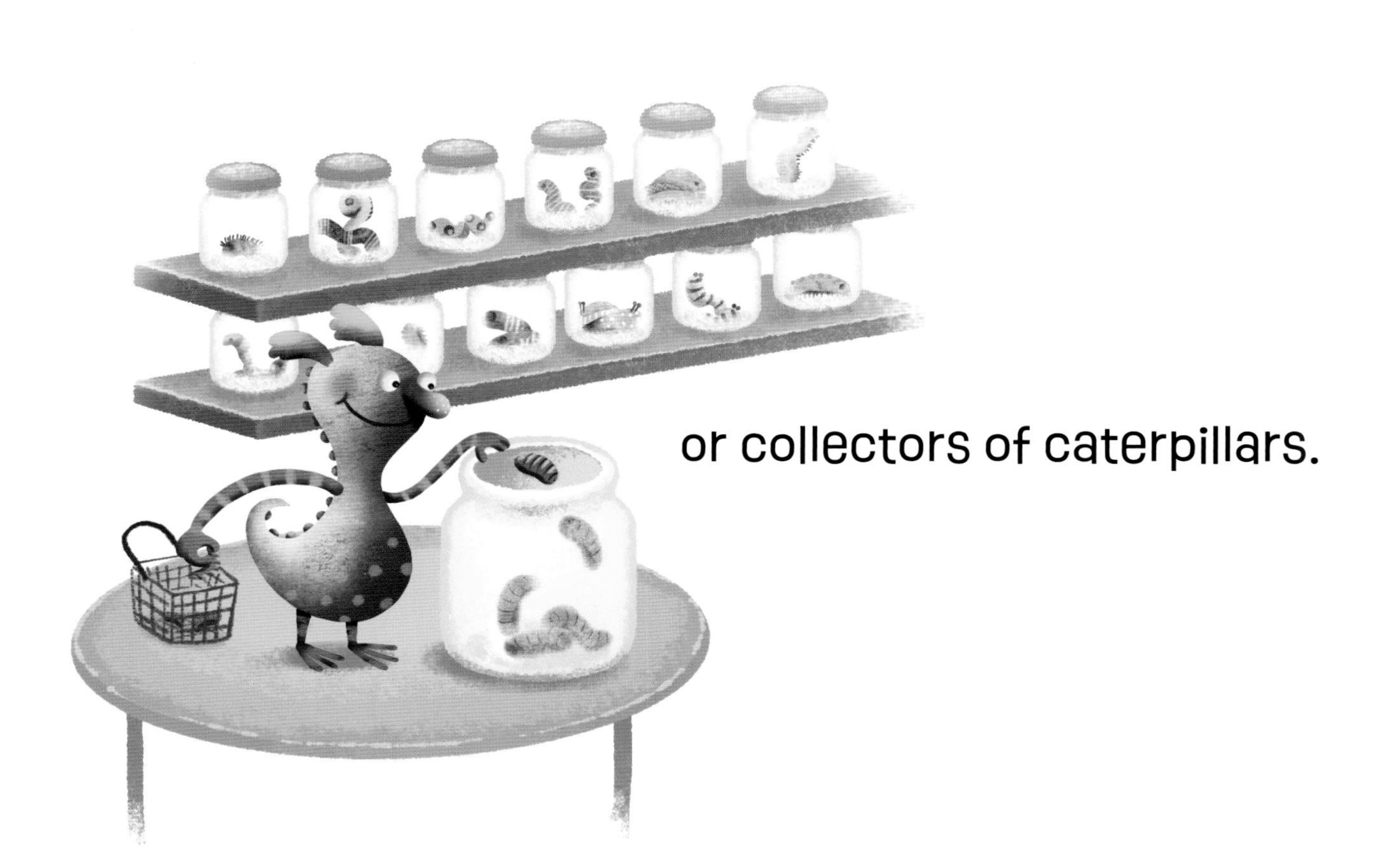

or collectors of caterpillars.

Yes, **anyone** can be a mensch.

It's easy to be kind.
It's easy to do the right thing.

Well, most of the time.

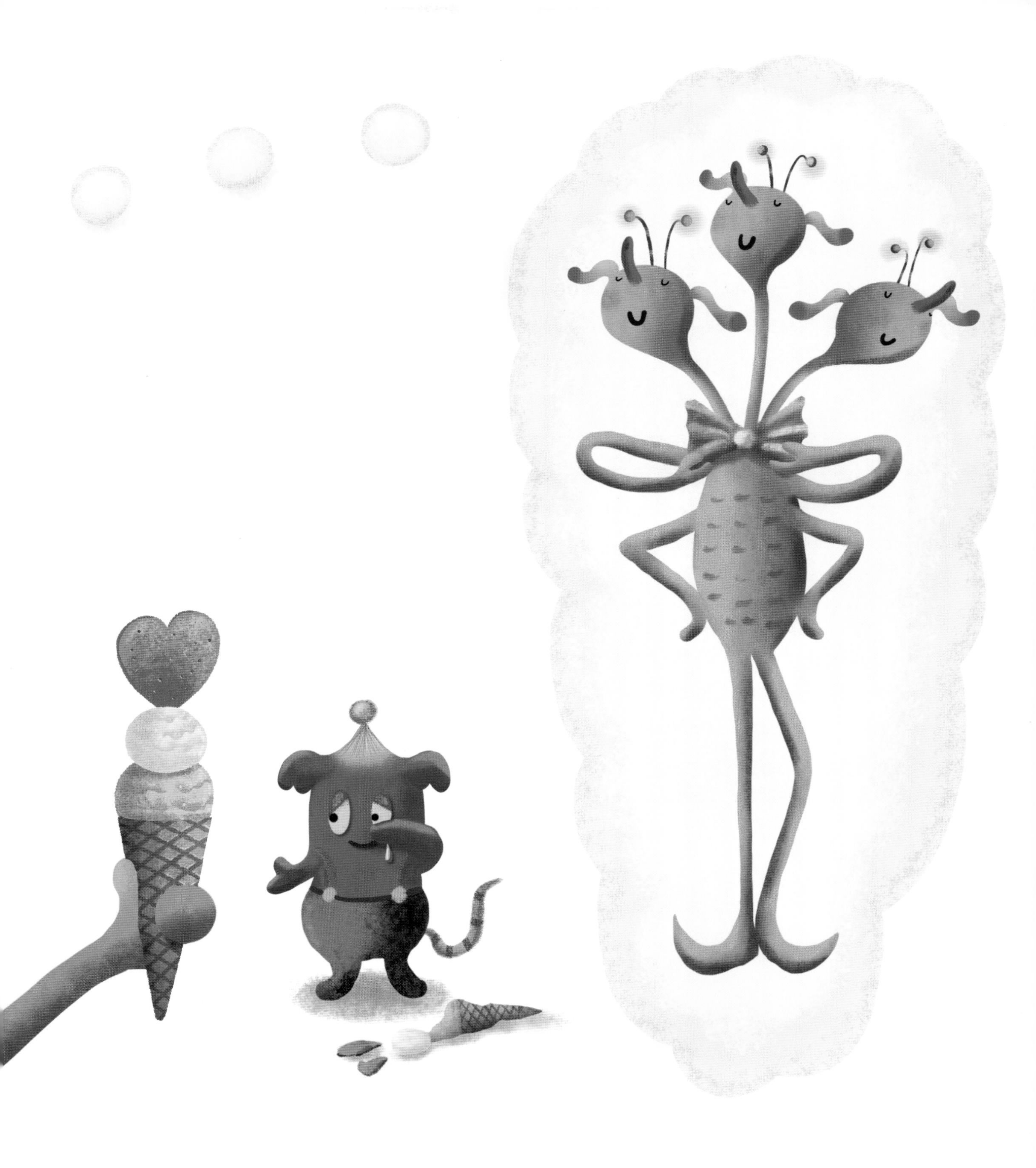

And even when it's not easy,
being a mensch makes us feel ten feet tall!

Mensches are good neighbors,
greeting everyone with a warm smile
and a friendly ***HOWL-o.***

Please, thank you, and
excuse me are also
good mensch words.

Café
Mud Café

A mensch may
be helpful in
finding things
that are lost,

fixing things that
are broken,

and lending a helping hand.

Even the smallest acts of kindness
can make a big difference.

Helping to protect the Earth
and all its creatures is a very
menschy thing to do.

Mensches care
and share.

But we don't stare—
not with one eye,
and not with five.

Being a monster is fun
(so, so, **so fun!**) . . .

A
B
C
Who is the most flexible?
M
Shriekling Contest

. . . but even little monsters
treat teachers with respect,

and families with kindness.

Caring for the sick is a
clear menschy sign.

And mensches always
remember to sneeze
and cough into a tissue
or an elbow, keeping our
germs to ourselves!

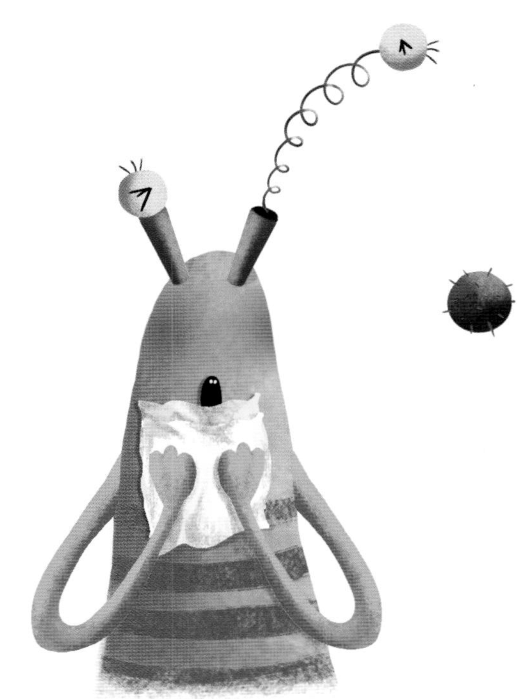

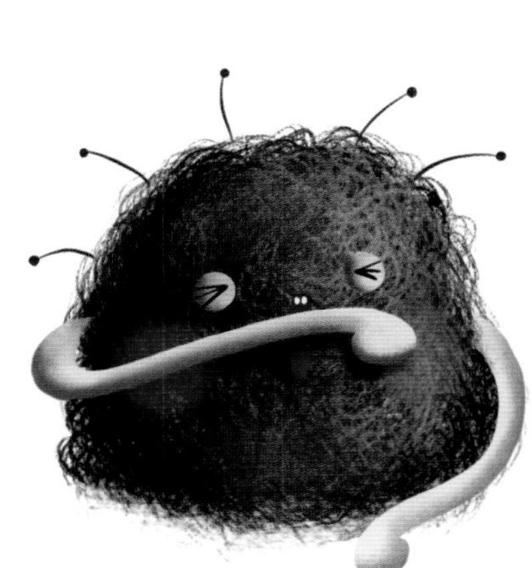

When Fridays roll around,
mensches pitch in to prepare for Shabbat:

setting the table,
taking care of the cobwebs,
or braiding the challah.

That makes Shabbat more
fun for everyone.

Then a mensch—or a whole
mensch family—can enjoy some
quiet time. Yes, quiet!

Even monsters sometimes
need quiet. And even monsters
can be mensches.

What kind of mensch
will *you* be?

To Julian, a mensch-in-training, with much love. — LK

For my dearest daughter, Kinu. — SY

Apples & Honey Press
An Imprint of Behrman House Publishers
Millburn, New Jersey 07041
www.applesandhoneypress.com

ISBN 978-1-68115-590-6

Library of Congress Cataloging-in-Publication Data

Names: Kimmelman, Leslie, author. | Yoshikawa, Sachiko, illustrator.
Title: How to be a mensch / by A. Monster as told to Leslie Kimmelman ; illustrated by Sachiko Yoshikawa.
Description: Millburn, New Jersey : Apples & Honey Press, [2022] | Audience: Ages 3-6. | Audience: Grades K-1. | Summary: "A fun romp through a neighborhood where even monsters can be mensches"-- Provided by publisher.
Identifiers: LCCN 2021050422 | ISBN 9781681155906 (hardcover)
Subjects: CYAC: Conduct of life--Fiction. | Monsters--Fiction. | LCGFT: Picture books.
Classification: LCC PZ7.K56493 Ho 2022 | DDC [E]--dc23
LC record available at https://lccn.loc.gov/2021050422

Design by Alexandra N. Segal
Edited by Aviva Gutnick and Ann D. Koffsky
Printed in China

9 8 7 6 5 4 3 2 1

0124/B2470/A4